Freckleface

Julianne Moore

Strawberry

illustrated by **LeUyen Pham**

BLOOMSBURY
CHILDREN'S
BOOKS

Typeset in Bodoni Six Book and Minya Nouvelle
Illustrations rendered with a Japanese brush pen and digitally colored
Book design by Donna Mark

Published by Bloomsbury U.S.A. Children's Books
175 Fifth Avenue, New York, NY 10010

Library of Congress Cataloging-in-Publication Data
Moore, Julianne.
Freckleface Strawberry / Julianne Moore ;
illustrated by LeUyen Pham.—1st U.S. ed.
p.   cm.
Summary: Freckleface Strawberry is just like everyone else,
except that she has red hair and freckles, but when she tries to hide who she is,
she learns about true friendship and accepting yourself just as you are.
ISBN-13: 978-1-59990-107-7 • ISBN-10: 1-59990-107-2 (hardcover)
ISBN-13: 978-1-59990-137-4 • ISBN-10: 1-59990-137-4 (reinforced)
[1. Freckles—Fiction. 2. Self-acceptance—Fiction. 3. Friendship—Fiction.]
I. Pham, LeUyen, ill. II. Title.
PZ7.M78635Fr 2007   [E]—dc22   2006102608

First U.S. Edition 2007
Printed in China by C&C offset printing Co.Ltd., Shenzhen, Guangdong.
3 5 7 9 10 8 6 4 (hardcover)
3 5 7 9 10 8 6 4 2 (reinforced)

All papers used by Bloomsbury U.S.A. are natural, recyclable products
made from wood grown in well-managed forests. The manufacturing processes
conform to the environmental regulations of the country of origin.

To Cal and Liv—
my own little, not-so-freckled
strawberries
—J. M.

To Melanie—
a constant happy spot in my life
—L. P.

Once upon a time there was a little girl who was just like everybody else.

She was seven.

Look! I lost another tooth!

She was short.

She could ride a bike.

She was just like everybody else
except for one thing.

She had red hair.

And something worse . . .

FRECKLES!

How she got them was a mystery.

Her father didn't have freckles.
Her mother didn't have freckles.
Her sister didn't have freckles.

Her baby brother—
oh, yeah. He had freckles,
but he was just a baby.

People always had something to say
about her freckles.

But most of the time
they just said:

Freckleface Strawberry felt really bad.
She needed to get rid of her freckles fast.

She tried scrubbing them.

Get out of the bathroom!

She tried lemon juice.

She even tried markers,
but her mom got mad.

Nothing worked.

If she couldn't make her freckles go away,
she would just have to hide.

It worked!

All her freckles were gone.

It worked so well, she started wearing it to school.

It worked so well, nobody said anything
about her freckles anymore.

It worked so well, none of her friends
knew where she was.

Have you seen her?

She's short, and she
can ride a bike.

She has freckles
all over her body.

Freckleface Strawberry
was kind of sad. And hot.
And a little itchy.

After school, at the playground, she was lonely. Everybody was playing except for Freckleface Strawberry. She was sitting in the shade wishing she wasn't so hot.

Somebody tugged on her shirt.

It was a baby. Freckleface
Strawberry knew about babies
because of her little brother.

The baby started to laugh.

She laughed and laughed and laughed.

She was just glad she wasn't so hot anymore.
Or itchy.

Suddenly Freckleface Strawberry
heard some familiar voices:

Freckleface Strawberry,
go down the slide with me!

Freckleface Strawberry,
you have to meet the new girl.
She wears a ski mask all the time.

Freckleface Strawberry,
were you sick?

Freckleface Strawberry, we missed you!

Freckleface Strawberry smiled so wide,
she thought she would crack open.

She wasn't hot.
She wasn't itchy.
And she wasn't sad anymore.

Who cared about having a million freckles
when she had a million friends?

And maybe that mom was right and
her freckles would go away a little.

And Freckleface Strawberry really was like everybody else—she grew up.

And her freckles . . .

. . . DID NOT GO AWAY!

But somehow, she didn't care so much after all.

In fact, she lived happily ever after.